Tilly the Trickster

By
Molly
Shannon

Illustrated by
Ard
Hoyt

ABRAMS BOOKS FOR YOUNG READERS · NEW YORK

ARTIST'S NOTE

I created the illustrations using watercolor paints on Arches hot press watercolor paper and finished in ink. I love the inking—it is my dessert and always best if saved for last.

Cataloging-in-Publication Data has been applied for and may be obtained from the Library of Congress.
ISBN: 978-1-4197-0030-9

Text copyright © 2011 Molly Shannon
Illustrations copyright © 2011 Ard Hoyt
Book design by Maria T. Middleton

Printed and bound in Mexico
10 9 8 7 6 5 4 3 2

Abrams Books for Young Readers are available at special discounts when purchased in quantity for premiums and promotions as well as fundraising or educational use. Special editions can also be created to specification. For details, contact specialsales@abramsbooks.com or the address below.

ABRAMS
THE ART OF BOOKS SINCE 1949
115 West 18th Street
New York, NY 10011
www.abramsbooks.com

To Stella and Nolan—
my very own little tricksters.

—M. S.

To my friend George Mitchel for his vision
of good things to come and many laughs.

—A. H.

Today is the perfect day for tricks. I love, **love, love** to play tricks. First, I hop out of my pj's and pull on my school clothes superfast.

Then, I hop back into bed and pretend to be sound asleep. I don't put my favorite red shoes on yet, because I do NOT like shoes in my bed!

"Tilly, you're still in bed? Hurry up! Get out of your pajamas!" Mommy says as she walks in my room.

"Surprise!" I shout,
throwing back the covers.
"Look, I'm already dressed
for school."
"Tilly, you little
TRiCKSTER!"
Mommy says.

During breakfast, Daddy says, "I'm thirsty. Can some-one get me a glass of water?"

"I will!" I shout.

First, I grab a paper cup from the cupboard.

Then, I carefully poke a hole in the side of the cup with a pencil. If this ever-so-clever trick works, water will spill through the hole when Daddy tips the cup to take a drink.

"Here, Daddy! Have some water," I say.

"My cup is leaking! I'm all **WET!**" Daddy says.

"Tricked you!" I squeal.

Daddy does not look happy.

Suddenly, Peppermint, our dog, comes charging in to see what's going on. The floor is so **slip-slip-slippery** from the water that Peppermint goes sliding across the floor until . . .

"No more tricks, Tilly! That wasn't funny. Look at this mess,"
Mommy says. But this trick was even funnier than I planned.

I put on my favorite red shoes and go to the bus stop. While waiting for my school bus with my classmates, I get in the mood for more mischief! I think of the perfect trick.

I say, "Hey, guys, the bus already came. You missed it. I guess you need to walk to school."

My friends fall for the trick and start walking to school! Some of them even run because they're afraid they'll be late.

When the bus finally comes, I'm **TiCkLED** that I get it all to myself.

At school, I decide to play a SNEAKY trick on my music teacher, Mrs. Mooney.

I say, "Mrs. Mooney, I made some strawberry candy. It's so delicious. Would you like to try some?"

"How delightful, Tilly!" Mrs. Mooney says.

She has no idea that the candy is not strawberry flavored. It's cinnamon. And it's **hot, hot, hot!**

"HELP! My mouth is on fire! I need water!"
Mrs. Mooney yells.

Mrs. Mooney did NOT think my trick was funny. The principal did NOT think my trick was funny. And Mommy and Daddy did NOT think my trick was funny, either.

"Mr. and Mrs. Callahan, your daughter **Tilly** is quite the **TRiCKSTeR!** I am not pleased with her petty little pranks!" the principal says.

I'm sent home for the rest of the day. I play a teeny-tiny trick and pretend like I'm sad about being sent home, but really . . .

But then Mommy and Daddy bring me home and tell me:

1) I need to calm my body down. (They tell me that a lot.)

2) No special treats for the rest of the day.

3) I have to spend quiet time in my room thinking about how NAUGHTY I've been.

Life is so dreadfully boring without tricks.

But then I get an idea. I have just one more trick I want to play today. My little brother, Teddy, **loves, loves, loves** cookies. His favorites are the ones with the yummy creamy center.

First, I sneak out of my bedroom, grab the toothpaste from the bathroom, and slink into the kitchen, where I grab a cookie. Then, I twist the top off the cookie, remove the creamy white center with my fingers, and replace it with YUCKY white toothpaste.

"Hey, Teddy," I say. "Here's one of your favorite cookies."

Teddy puts the whole cookie in his mouth and starts to chew. Suddenly, his face turns green.

Teddy spits out the cookie and it lands all over my FAVORITE RED SHOES!

"**YUCK!**" I scream. My trick was supposed to be funny, not get my shoes dirty.

Then Teddy tells me he has a tummy ache. My trick wasn't supposed to make Teddy get a tummy ache.

Maybe I shouldn't be such a TRiCKSTER?

I clean up the mess I've made with my trick and put my favorite red shoes outside to dry.

Later that night, after bath time, it starts raining really hard. Mommy notices my red shoes are still outside.

"Oh no, Tilly! Your shoes are soaking wet," Mommy says.

"Here, put on your nice, cozy slippers instead," Daddy says.
I put on the slippers. Suddenly, I feel something COLD
and **SQUISHY** under my toes.
My slippers are filled with shaving cream!

"We **TRiCKED** you, **Tilly!**"
my family yells.

They laugh and laugh.

After we wash off my feet, Mommy and Daddy tuck me into bed.

"Tonight was fun, but no more tricks.
OK, Tilly?" Mommy says.

"OK, Mommy. OK, Daddy," I say. "No more tricks . . ."

. . . until tomorrow.